This book belongs

_____

Published by Ladybird Books Ltd
80 Strand London WC2R 0RL
A Penguin Company

13 15 17 19 20 18 16 14

Printed in Italy

The Pied Piper
of Hamelin

illustrated by John Holder

Ladybird

Once upon a time, there was a beautiful little town called Hamelin.

The people of Hamelin were all very happy, until the day the rats came.

Thousands of rats came to Hamelin. There were big rats and little rats, thin rats and fat rats. There were rats in all the houses and rats in all the shops.

"There are rats on my table!"
said one man.

"There are rats under my chair!"
said another.

"There are rats in my kitchen!"
called one woman.

"There are rats in my bed!"
called another.

"There are rats all over the house!" called a little boy.

"Make these rats go away!" called a little girl.

The people of Hamelin went to see the mayor.

"Get rid of these rats!" they shouted.

"What can I do?" said the mayor. "There are rats in my house, too. I can't get rid of them."

But the people said, "You must make all the rats go away. If you don't make them go away we will choose another mayor."

Then one day, a stranger went to see the mayor. He was dressed in red and yellow. In his hand he carried a pipe.

"I am the Pied Piper," said the stranger, "and I can make the rats go away."

The mayor said, "If you can make these rats go away, I will give you lots of money."

"Very well," said the Pied Piper. "But don't forget your promise."

Then the Pied Piper went into the streets of Hamelin and began to play a strange tune.

19

The rats heard the tune and stopped what they were doing.

Suddenly, one rat ran after the Pied Piper. Then another rat ran after him. And another. Soon, all the rats ran after the Pied Piper.

The Pied Piper walked towards the river, still playing the strange tune on his pipe. The rats followed him and jumped into the river. And that was the end of the rats.

23

The Pied Piper went back to see the mayor.

"The rats have all gone," he said. "Please give me the money you promised me."

"No," said the mayor. "I have no money to give you."

25

"If you don't give me the money," said the Pied Piper, "I will play another tune, and you will not be so happy then."

"You can do what you like," said the mayor.

So the Pied Piper went out into the streets and began to play another tune.

In all the houses and in all the streets, the children stopped playing. Then, one by one, they ran after the Pied Piper.

The people of Hamelin called to the children to stop, but the children didn't hear. They followed the Pied Piper through the streets and over the river.

They followed the Pied Piper out of the town and up a mountain.

Suddenly, the mountain opened up and the Pied Piper went inside. The children followed him. Inside the mountain was a beautiful land full of trees and flowers and birds.

But one little boy had hurt his leg
and he couldn't keep up with the
other children. He saw his friends
go into the mountain, but he was
too late to follow them.

The little boy went back to the town and went to see the mayor.

"My friends are inside the mountain with the Pied Piper," he said. "They will never come back."

The people of Hamelin were
very unhappy.

"Where are our children?" they
shouted to the mayor. "You must
go and find them."

So the mayor went to look for the children. He looked for years and years and years. He is still looking for them now.